Be Careful, Kangaroo!

based on text by Deirdre Langeland

Illustrated by Frank Ordaz

For Sasha, who explored Australia with me, and for my parents, just because. — D.L.

For my son Isaac, who wants to draw kangaroos. — F.O.

Book design: Marcin D. Pilchowski
Editor: Laura Gates Galvin
Editorial assistance: Chelsea Shriver

First Edition 2003
10 9 8 7 6 5 4 3 2 1
Printed in China

Acknowledgments:
　　　　Our very special thanks to Peggy and Mike McKelvey of the Pelican Lagoon Research and Wildlife Centre on Kangaroo Island for their review and guidance. Thanks also to Rooby and Jumper, the Centre's resident 'roos, for being such good models!

Library of Congress Cataloging-in-Publication Data is on file with the publisher and the Library of Congress.

Be Careful, Kangaroo!

based on text by Deirdre Langeland

Illustrated by Frank Ordaz

A note to the reader:
Throughout this story you will see words in **bold letters**. There is more information about these words in the glossary. The glossary is in the back of the book.

Late one hot afternoon, a young kangaroo rests in the shade with his family. When the sun sets, Kangaroo will look for food.

Kangaroo hears

thunder. His family

hears thunder, too.

A storm is coming!

Soon the sun sets. Other animals in the **forest** come out to eat. *Boom!* More thunder crashes.

The sky turns darker. It is windy. The air turns cool. Now Kangaroo and his family eat and drink.

Kangaroo sips water.
There is something
in the water. It is a
platypus!

Crash! Kangaroo leaps away. **Lightning** hits a tree. A small fire starts!

Soon the fire is
big! Flames are all
around. Where is
Kangaroo's mother?

The rain comes.
The rain puts out
the fire. Kangaroo
is safe now. But
Kangaroo needs to
find his mother.

Soon Kangaroo sees his mother! He is happy to be back in her **pouch**. She is happy, too.

Kangaroo and his family eat. Other animals eat, too.

Kangaroo stays close to his mother. He does not want to lose her again!

Glossary

Forest: a wooded land covering a large area.

Lightning: a flash of light caused by a charge of electricity in the atmosphere.

Platypus: a small mammal that looks like a duck.

Pouch: a pocket in a kangaroo's stomach used for carrying a baby kangaroo, also known as a joey.

Thunder: the sound that follows a flash of lightning.

Wilderness Facts
About the Kangaroo

The kangaroo in this story is based on a western gray kangaroo that can be found on a large island in South Australia called Kangaroo Island.

At its full height, the kangaroo stands between five and six feet tall and weighs between 50 and 120 pounds. Kangaroos have powerful hind legs and can travel at speeds up to 30 miles per hour and can leap some 30 feet!

Female kangaroos give birth to tiny, hairless babies, called "joeys." Joeys live in their mothers' pouches for almost one year until they grow fur and are big enough to start living outside the pouch. On average, kangaroos in the wild live for six to eight years.

Other animals that live in an Australian mallee forest:

Cockatoos

Fairy penguins

Platypus

Possums

Sea lions

Wallabies